Cuttin' the Rug
Under
the Moonlit Sky

Doubleday

New York London Toronto Sydney Auckland

Cuttin' the Rug Under the Moonlit Sky

Stories and Drawings About
a Bunch of Women Named Mae

Sharony Andrews Green

AN ANCHOR BOOK
PUBLISHED BY DOUBLEDAY
a division of Bantam Doubleday Dell Publishing Group, Inc.
1540 Broadway, New York, New York 10036

ANCHOR BOOKS, DOUBLEDAY, and the portrayal of an anchor
are trademarks of Doubleday, a division of
Bantam Doubleday Dell Publishing Group, Inc.

Book design by Jennifer Ann Daddio

Library of Congress Cataloging-in-Publication Data
Green, Sharony Andrews.
Cuttin' the rug under the moonlit sky: stories and drawings about a bunch of women named
Mae / Sharony Andrews Green. — 1st Anchor Books ed.
p.   cm.
1. Afro-American women — Anecdotes.   2. Afro-American women — Portraits.
3. Afro-American women — Poetry.   4. Green, Sharony Andrews — Family —
Anecdotes.   5. Green, Sharony Andrews — Family — Poetry.   6. Green, Sharony
Andrews — Friends and associates — Anecdotes.   7. Green, Sharony Andrews —
Friends and associates — Poetry.   8. Mae (Name) — Anecdotes.   9. Mae
(Name) — Poetry.   I. Title.   II. Title: Cuttin' the rug under the moonlit sky.
E185.96.G75   1997
973'.0496073 — DC21
96-47859
CIP

ISBN 0-385-48840-8
Copyright © 1997 by Sharony Andrews Green
All Rights Reserved
Printed in the United States of America
First Anchor Books Edition: August 1997

1   3   5   7   9   10   8   6   4   2

Acknowledgments

"Corrine Mae" and "Claudine Mae" have appeared in *The Snail's Pace Review*.

Special thanks to: the House Buddha and coffee compotator, Jeffrey Renaud; Diana Pardo; Jacqui Colyer; my husband, Grant Green "Uncle Peanut Butter" Jr.; Patrice Hendricks; Andrea Sparks; the staff at Detroit Public Library; SARK; Roy Zarruchi; Carolyn Page; Nancy Farrell; Sheila Nudd; Kathy and Sarah Anderson; Linda Cousins; Evantheia Schibsted; my Beau Brummel agent Julie Castiglia; my editor Charlie Conrad; my publisher Martha Levin; my mama, the lovely Estella Andrews; God, my Angel Mae, and everyone who gave me encouragement when this was only a handmade book tied with polka-dot ribbon.

To Magda, Louella, Melcina, May Dell,
and all the Maes I have known before,
given name or otherwise,
in real life or spirit.

In special memory of Mae Belle Washington
Birthplace: Hahira, Georgia
February 23, 1944—August 17, 1996

When I was growing up, my Greek grandmother would sometimes call me Evantheia Mou. Hearing my grandmother say it used to make me want to snuggle up under her big breasts. It's the kind of association that gets you right in the gut.

— Evantheia Schibsted

*This is a book about
a bunch of women
named Mae.*

They all have stories to tell, but they don't tell them. The voices
that do are anonymous, but familiar. They are the voices of the
women in my life: grandmas, mamas, god-mamas, aunts,
cousins, sisters, sister-girls, girlfriends, kinfolk, or kinspirit,
some real, some imaginary. Their voices express a universal
message of endurance, their yesterdays whisper a certain
rhythm and strength.

Some of the Maes are from the early part of the
twentieth century when a woman's place was in the house; others
are from our more modern day when a woman could certainly
make the world her home. She is the woman you've known and
didn't know you did — that school crossing guard, that lady at
the bus stop, that attorney, that woman doing day work in your
uncle's house. And that woman in love songs famous people sing
about.

The first Mae in my life was my maternal grandmother,

Lillie Mae Golden Earvin. She was born in Belzoni, Mississippi, in 1929. I also have some Maes on my father's side, including a great-aunt named Lottie Mae and the woman who named me, my Aunt Willie Mae.

There is something about adding Mae to a name that gives it a special punch. When I was coming up, there was from time to time an authority figure in my life who would add the name Mae to my name. This was usually a teacher. Always female. Probably with roots in the South. If she wanted me to, for example, take a seat, this teacher would say, "Sharony. Sharony Mae." Her tone, and the adding of this name, offered a kinship. A kinship with our people. A kinship with all the women who had gone before both her and me. A kinship with a time when almost any adult in the neighborhood, in the absence of your parent, could get you on the road to obedience with a harsh word. Or a good behind-whupping.

When she would say, "Sharony Mae," I knew it was time to sit down.

Now there are the Maes whose names carry a y instead of an e like the late blues-jazz singer Big Maybelle. Or the country music singer Maybelle Carter. I also know of a May Dell. She was the mother of Gloria "Gigi" Braynon Watson, one of my best sources when I was a reporter in Miami. Gigi studied at the Sorbonne in Paris in the 1960s and went on to become the first black French teacher in Miami. Mother May Dell Braynon was a petite, church-goin' woman who always had a smile for everyone. Ask her how she was doing and she'd always respond, "I'm fine as silver satin wine!" Rain or shine, May Dell was fine.

My urge to celebrate Maes came about five years ago when I went to Jackson Hole, Wyoming, for a retreat sponsored by the Journalism and Women Symposium. Every year JAWS picks a spot out West where female journalists from around the world can rub elbows with the pioneers in the business, whine about their respective newsrooms, and empower themselves by hiking, whitewater rafting, and a good cry over Thelma & Louise.

My good friend Jacqui came along with the intention of using the retreat as a way to work on her doctoral thesis. But we ended up talking late into the night about books, history, and Jacqui's niece, Carla, who was five years old at the time. Carla would always dial Jacqui's number and say, "Hey, Jacqui Mae!" And Jacqui would respond, "Hey, Carla Mae!" This Mae stuff was something Jacqui — who had come from a long line of Maes, including a Hessie Mae, a Jessie Mae, a Flossie Mae, and her mother, a Hester Mae — started. And Carla took note. Along with being a common name for many women a couple of generations ago Mae has also been known to be a term of endearment. Get to know and love a person long enough and you might just hear the word "Mae" roll off your tongue. It's like giving someone a big hug. For example, I have a friend named Marcy. She's white. I'm black.

One day she said something — what she said I don't know, can't remember — that made me say, "Oh, Marcy Mae!" She didn't totally get it, but just adding Mae after her name let her know that I really loved having her in my life.

While in Wyoming, Jacqui and I tried to name all of the famous Maes we could, including the late actress Mae West of "Come up and see me sometime" fame. The astronaut Mae Jemison. And the singer Tina Turner. We noted how they were all in some way ground-breakers. Mae West use to cleverly deliver her lines to convey a double meaning, often parodying attitudes on sex to escape the wrath of motion picture censors in the 1930s. Turner, who was born Anna Mae Bullock in Nutbush, Tennessee, rose from being a 1960s soul queen in an abusive relationship to a rock-pop legend in the 1980s. Jemison had humble beginnings in Chicago and went on to become the first black female astronaut in the 1990s.

The name Mae makes one feel safe. Nurtured. I have heard my grandfather drop Lillie from my grandma's name and just say, "Mae." He does this when he's a little under the weather or when he wants her to fix him a plate of food. He just whimpers, "Mae." It's like calling out for mama.

Of late, I have learned of international Maes like the Canadian folk-jazz singer Mae Moore, who once snatched the best musicians she could find and stole away to a rural house by the sea to record an album. And the Singapore-born and London-raised violinist Vanessa Mae Vanakorn

Nicholson, who uses a techno acoustic fusion doorway to present the greats like Beethoven, Tchaikovsky, and Mozart. I believe all of these women might be showing the way because their very names give permission: Mae. Or May.

Mae Be. Maybe. Maybe the name Mae gives these black women, the black woman, women, people, hope.

I have also discovered geographical Maes like Mae Hong Son, a town in northwest Thailand. Or May Pen in Jamaica. I have read of a Russian Mae from Philly, a Seminole Indian Mae from Florida. Maes are everywhere, even in song. Blues singer John Lee Hooker has a catalog that includes an _Anna Mae,_ a _Rosie Mae,_ and a _Stella Mae._ There is also a Mae in _Sadie,_ the 1970s ode to the black mother by the Spinners. She creeps up in the part of the song where the backup guys croon, "Sa-die, don't-cha know we love ya, Sweet Sadie," prompting the lead singer to let go and just moan, "Sa-die Ma-aae." Just adding Mae to the name made the song more accessible and took it somewhere higher.

Maes seem to crop up everywhere. On television, there was the Elly May character in _The Beverly Hillbillies._ There are Maes in literature. Take Louisa May Alcott, the leading children's book writer during the nineteenth century, best known for _Little Women._ Or the late May Sarton, one of my favorite contemporary author-poets. Now, some folks may not remember this — because Zora Neale Hurston makes mention of it just once — but the spunky heroine Janie Crawford in Hurston's highly acclaimed novel *Their Eyes Were Watching God* was a Janie Mae. And then there are the Maes in film. I'll never forget that scene in Spike Lee's *School Daze* when Half-Pint is chastised for being a virgin, a fact he disputes by announcing that he "did it" once — with a Susie Mae in high school. Some great character actors also bore the name May, like Massachusetts-born Edna May Oliver and Dame May Whitty, a native of Liverpool, England, both of whom were highly regarded on stage and on screen in the early part of this century. The name has even made a presence in the paintings of great artists. Consider the French artist Henri Toulouse-Lautrec, whose favorite subjects were the entertainers, singers, and dancers in the Montmartre nightclub district of Paris. Among the many entertainers he immortalized on posters in the late 1880s was a woman named May Belfort. And May has stepped up to the world of high fashion, for one has been able to purchase a pair of blue leather sandals by the Australia-based shoemaker Donna May Bolinger at Barneys.

Mae has been knitted into racial politics: one of the four black girls killed in the 1963 church bombing in Alabama was an Addie Mae. Maes have even been stitched into the economic fabric of this country. Witness Fannie Mae, Ginnie Mae, and Sallie Mae.

American icons have come from the wombs of Maes. Elvis's grandmother is a Minnie Mae and the voice of Betty Boop was Mae Questal. May is so cool she has a month, even a day, named after her. And also she is royalty, for we honor the May Queen.

I had a lot of fun working on this book. It was a departure from the harder-edge writing I've done as a journalist over the past eight years. And it gave me a chance to mix words with my first love: art. I started drawing when I was in elementary school during the 1970s, under the tutelage of my art teacher, Miss Bader. She was a rather determined woman of high voice and foreign beginnings who encouraged me to draw and paint. She entered my work in all kinds of contests. (I can still remember pasting construction paper cutouts of banal childhood proverbs like "Brush Your Teeth Every Day to Prevent Tooth Decay" to poster board for the annual dental association competition.) Once she made me stay after school every day for a whole week to draw a picture of my family for a national contest sponsored by Crayola crayons and Reader's Digest. I remember falling asleep with an oil pastel in my hand, but the drawing won me $125. The eleven-year-old in me wanted to frame the check, but my daddy thought the bank was a better place for it.

Five years ago in Miami Beach, I had another teacher, a quirky man named Tomata du Plenty. There were just four adults in the class and Tomata would have us sitting on sidewalks on Lincoln Road, at tables in Cuban cafés, and on stools in dive pubs, drawing and writing in journals. It was Tomata who gave me a set of watercolors to do my end-of-the-class project, a six-panel cartoon on my fondness for the name Mae.

Except for the mindless scribbles in my reporter's notebook, another three years passed before I drew again.

It happened at Villa Montalvo, an artists' colony in Saratoga, California, where I was working on a biography about my husband's dad, the late jazz guitarist Grant Green. Over potluck dinners, I got to know the other artists-in-residence, the "real" artists, folks with formal training who had their works presented in shows and museums far and wide. One was a middle-aged guy from Boston with spiked hair; another was a young woman from Orlando who spotted the love of her life sitting on the villa's estate below her window; and the other was a Mexican woman who made an incredible flan. When I wasn't working on the jazz book, I was sneaking over to their studios, where I was tolerated or given "tools" — chalk and crayons — to play with.

I graduated to markers in no time. A set that cost $1.99 from a Safeway grocery store produced the foundation for my first four Maes: Carrie Mae, Lorraine Mae, Freda Mae, and Ruthie Mae. The creating took me back to simpler times when I was a kid, when I used to get up early on Saturday mornings with my markers and a bowl of cereal and draw. I loved to draw people, especially women who could be considered pretend ancestors of the women I want you to meet now, my Maes.

There are all kinds of ways to read this book, straight through or in any order you fancy. But the best time to read these stories is probably those moments when you're feeling a little bummed. Just open it and find a Mae who's trying to figure it out, too. That's what I'm planning to do. I may even put on a John Lee Hooker album for us to dance to, too.

—S.A.G.

Cuttin' the Rug
Under
the Moonlit Sky

Carrie Mae

Carrie Mae left home when she was 14,
looking for love north of the Mississippi line.
She found Grover and his three babies.
Cooked, cleaned, and loved like a good woman did,
but Grover up and left her with those babies.
People say, "Carrie, give 'em to the state.
They mammy been dead." But Carrie said no.
She said in Africa it took a whole village to raise a child.
And as far as she was concerned, she was just a new hut
to keep them fed and warm.
Sometimes Miss Carrie sings herself to sleep at night,
keeping those babies warm.

Lorraine Mae

Lorraine got plans now.
Mae gon' open up her a restaurant one day.
Say she won't be working for white people
all her life. Say she even know
what the menu look like:
Tasty turnip greens.
Sweet iced tea.
Buttery sweet potato pie.
Potato salad. Honey baby-back ribs
with extra sauce on the side.
And a big pan of her grandma's cornbread
fried on top of the stove.
This is what Lorraine Mae say she gon' do.
I overheard her talkin' 'bout it
in the powder room.

They named Freda Mae after Grandma Odessa's sister and Freda didn't mind too much 'cuz she was into the retro thing anyway. Graduated tops in her class back home in Greenville, but figured the big city was more to her liking, so she tossed her A&T application and headed north to Cambridge so she could — when she felt like it — scoot up to Montreal or down to the Big Apple. Mama says she's going to be an engineer one day, tho' I dunno. Freda's always been known to do things her way. I s'pose she might end up in France, drinking fancy coffee in some outdoor café between teaching classes at the Sorbonne, 'cuz Freda's got it like that. Always has.

Freda Mae

Ella Mae

Ella Mae was just 13
when Bruce Tinker caught her eye.
By the age of 17, she had four kids by him,
but he died. "Diphtheria," the doctor say.
Anyway
Ella had to feed those kids,
but she didn't know how.
All she knew is that they was hungry now,
so she took 'em over to Mr. and Mrs. Robinson's house
and said, "Let 'em work, but please feed 'em 'til I get back."
And off those kids went into the fields, pickin' pole beans
while they mama headed off
in another direction to figure things out.
Ella tried washing and ironing, but she found
the dollars was in dancing.
And dance Ella Mae did, thinking 'bout her kids.
Polly say Ella dance real good, too.

Odessa Mae

Odessa Mae sneaked out the schoolyard
with Mick Junior and headed for the forest
back there behind Ole Man Dawson's mill.
And there Odessa let Mick Junior lay her down
on a bed of wildflowers
and whisper sweet nothings in her ear.
Mama say, "Odessa Mae,
keep your dress down
and your panties up
and never, never sit on a man's lap."
But Mick Junior's got Odessa Mae on fire
and it is with pleasure she pulls down her
thick white elastic bra strap
and Grandma's lacy purple slip
'cuz Mick Junior has reached under
and touched those
big brown thighs
Mama forgot how to feel.

Lucy Mae say she tired of the pens pushing and the clock ticking and the elevator stopping in her downtown office building. One day Lucy told her boss, "I quit. I'm going to Vermont." Boss Lady say, "Ain't no blacks in Vermont, Lucy Mae." But Lucy say, "There will be now." Boss Lady say, "But it's cold there, Lucy. Winters in Vermont are just dreadful. You sound like you running from something." Lucy say, "No, I'm running to something . . . to myself." And Lucy Mae took her purse, her Rolodex, and the classified section from the Burlington paper — she had already sent away for — and strutted on out. When she first arrived, she stayed at Miss Clara's hostel on Farmington and 'fore she know it, Miss Clara done took her to the country club, where she met a lotta people, including the other ten blacks in the state; two were students from Africa, seven were professors, and one was the state's beauty queen. "Imagine that," Lucy wrote us. "Miss Vermont black." Lucy say she waitressing between her women's studies classes. I think Lucy gon' be away for a while.

Lucy Mae

Cora Mae called her mama one day and said, "Ma, I'm having friends over tonight. Now, how was it that we made Grandma's sweet potato pie?" And Cora's ma said, "We?" 'Cuz best she remembered coming up, Cora never made no sweet potato pie. Her head was always stuck somewhere in a book, but Mama obliged Cora Mae and proceeded to say, "First you get your pie shell. 'Course you probably gon' buy it from the supermarket, but Mama always made her own. Then you get your potatoes, boil 'em & peel 'em, a cup of sugar, a stick of butter, some milk, and course some nutmeg, cinnamon, and a lil vanilla, and Sista Girl, I think you gon' be alright." Cora just smiled 'cuz there was no sense in telling Mama she needed actual measurements. Cora figured she'd just feel her way through it like all the women who'd come before her. And that she did. (Bob said Cora's pie was outasight, too.)

Cora Mae

Dorothy Mae had dreams she lost riding across the country in those big 18-wheelers next to Clyde. He said, "Sit real close, babe. I'm gon' take you places." All Dorothy remember was some pissy bathroom in Joe's truck stop when she got the first cramp. She bled so 'til Clyde thought she might not make it out of the hospital. It was a girl. Doctor said Dorothy would've never made it to full term and it was just as well because Dorothy was sick of Clyde and his lies and the house that never came. It was in Paducah, Kentucky, that Dorothy finally said, "Let me out!" And off she went into the sunset, clutching her tiny blue makeup case and her big yellow straw hat. They say Dorothy got her picket fence not too much long after. She's doin' hair now in a fine beauty shop the next town over.

Dorothy Mae

Donnie Mae worked hard in the Senator's big house and when she was finished for the week, she wanted her money. But Senator would always write her a check. Donnie would take Senator's check straight to Senator's bank up the street and get her cash right back. This she did every Friday. But one Friday she took Senator's check to the bank and the teller stepped away from the window. Donnie standing there, thinking 'bout that hot bath waiting and the bus she might miss if Miss Teller stay away too long. Miss Teller come back with the bank's president, who say Senator ain't had the funds to cover no check. And Donnie was plenty mad. But not as mad as the Senator, who had to be called and 'course he was quite embarrassed. Drove straight to the bank and yelled at Donnie for showing him up. And Donnie yelled back. Senator say, "You're fired!" Donnie say, "No, baby, I quit." Senator's wife called Donnie Mae for months. Said they children was crying for her and 'course no one did the linens like Donnie did. But Donnie did no more — especially not at the Senator's.

Donnie Mae

Mae Dean

Mae Dean still talkin' 'bout the revolution.
She was talkin' 'bout it around the time
that man flew that mosquito-lookin' plane
into the President's house on the hill.
I say, "Mae, you done missed the revolution.
We been that way before.
White folks ain't hearin' that stuff no more.
They fixin' to throw the quota out the door."
But Mae still talkin' 'bout the revolution.
Say, "Babies and black women dying from AIDS."
Mae say, "All of us need to be afraid."
She lights her sweet incense
and twists her soft nappy hair
while sitting on her faded orange thrift store chair,
watching the brothers run under her window at night,
carrying tv's.
Mae still talkin' 'bout the revolution.
"Have a seat," she say.
"Would you like a cup of my sweet potato-yam soup?"

Frances Mae

Frances Mae first heard her pappy playing
old Muddy Waters-type blues on his old guitar.
It was then Frances figured
she could play, too.
So she begged and begged her pappy
for a guitar. He bought her an old Harmony
from Mister Patterson's music store.
And Frances plinked and planked all night
to Charlie Parker solos.
'Fore she know it, the little ladies up yonder
at the church want her to play at the annual picnic.
Frances Mae don her red-checkered dress,
greased her legs down,
put a blue flower behind her ear,
and played her heart out.
They say after Frances made that gold record
she always found time to make it back
to play the church picnic every year.
Her pappy plenty proud.

Donna Mae Bea

Donna Mae Bea wonders how it's going to be
in that apartment without her Husband Ricky Lee.
He say Donna Mae want too much for him.
Say, "It's too much. A woman should just be."
That's according to Ricky Lee.
But Donna Mae see it another way.
And as long as her Citibank got a $5,000 limit,
she gon' get there one peanut butter sandwich
and a painting at a time.

Lillie Mae

Lillie Mae say the senior citizen building
is for old folks and she ain't old,
so she headed back to her own apartment
as her old husband sat down to play
a hand of cards.
She does visit,
carrying a bundle of collards in one hand,
her powder blue night bag in the other.
"Only on weekends," she announced
as she kissed her Ole Man on his bald head.
"Only on weekends."
Love be like that sometimes.

Annie Mae

Annie Mae, what choo say?
Gon' run a whorehouse
where men come to lay?
Gon' look for pretty girls
who've gone astray?
Annie Mae, what choo say?
Say, "The business go back
'to Christ's time."
Say, "Mind yours, I'll mind mine."
Annie Mae, what choo say?
Gon' reap the consequences
of your sinful deeds.
Best come with me and get on your knees,
and pray, Annie Mae.
Annie Mae say,
"Not today.
I got rent and my girls to pay.
But would you like a tall glass
of some sweet iced tea
to go with them tired knees?"
That's what Annie Mae say.

Claudine Mae Tillman knew she would be an artist one day. She was inspired by an art teacher in her elementary school named Ilsa. Ilsa say, "Paint, Claudine Mae. Paint." And Claudine paint. Ilsa say, "Draw, Claudine Mae. Draw." And Claudine drew. And drew. And paint and painted. Her teacher was a neat and cultured woman who wore fabrics with a high thread count and nameless perfumes from Paris. Her blonde hair was swept to the side and her blonde eyebrows were always plucked for strays. This was Ilsa's way. And Claudine took note. Claudine graduated summa cum laude with a master's in art history and specialty in Miró. But Claudine became a journalist. She wrote and did not draw. And did not paint. Years passed. She saw Ilsa again. She was ageless, Ilsa was. They renewed their friendship and went to museums together. Now, Claudine Mae was still the type of girl to notice small details, like the way Ilsa secured a little piece of satin cloth to the headrest of her car seat with two tiny safety pins. It was Ilsa's wish not to soil the headrest with the occasional oil from her still-blonde hair. In time, Ilsa say, "Come, Claudine Mae, to Germany with me. My sisters and I escaped the camps during the war, but my parents never made it out. What a story it would be for you to accompany me back to the camps. I would like to see again. Come, please." But Claudine was afraid. Did Ilsa want her to write the pain when she was now ready to draw and paint? Claudine lost contact with Ilsa. Missed opportunities, they call it.

Claudine Mae

The German journalist was looking for stories in the black community and the _Gazette_ sent him over to see Corrine Mae. Now, Corrine wasn't in no mood to be talkin' 'bout no revolutions, especially wit' no German, but she invited him into her loft and offered him a cup of tea. "Cinnamon, okay?" Corrine Mae say. The German say, "It is good." And they talked. They talked revolutions. On her shores. And his. They talked babies. Not hers. But his. They talked about her daddy who never made it home from the war. Nor did his. Before long the sun had set, but they still talkin'. The German lookin' at Corrine's brown breast and she know it. Her brown breast just hanging out of her thin purple dress already undone. They say that German loved Corrine all night. But she never returned his phone calls. The one time she tried a woman picked up and Corrine heard a baby's cry.

Corrine Mae

Rosie Mae

Johnny cooked, cleaned, and washed those babies
for Rosie Mae.
Johnny went to work early in the mornin' and came home
early in the evenin'
for Rosie Mae.
Johnny went outside and tilled the earth
and got those potatoes planted on time
for Rosie Mae.
Johnny got out the candles and the Nat King Cole records
and even stole a sunflower from Miss Stella's garden
for Rosie Mae.
This Johnny did. And he did it for Rosie Mae.
Rosie Mae doin' alright, y'all hear?
Rosie Mae doin' alright.

Stevie Mae

Stevie Mae lookin' all pretty.
Goin' to her fish fry with Joseph Purdy.
Stevie say she gon' cut the rug
under the moonlit sky
and close her eyes real tight
if Purdy
touches
her
thighs
'cuz Stevie loves
her
some
Purdy.

Flora Mae

Flora Mae looked at the brother
with the long nails laying beside her
and said to herself, "His love is good,
but I gots to love myself."
So she got up and kicked the can
in which he smoked his stuff
and went over to the mirror
where she pulled the extensions
out of her hair, one plait at a time.
This Flora did as she listened to the weatherman say,
"Partly cloudy. Highs in the 30s,
but we just may see some sun today."
Flora Mae turned up the radio to hear
'Reatha singing Ain't No Way.

Frankie Mae

(sung to the tune of any blues song. any one. just pick one.)

Frankie's got angels on her shoulders.
If she'd just look, Frankie Mae.
Frankie's got angels on her shoulders.
If she'd just look, that Frankie Mae.
Angels just flippin' and flappin',
carryin' on like that creek
back there babblin'.
Frankie's got angels on her shoulders.
Just turn your head, Frankie Mae.

Nona Mae

Nona Mae been on the phone all day.
Nona Mae be on the phone every day.
Nona Mae on the phone, talkin' trash
with her friends
about the babies' fathers
that done run away
and the phone bill she can't pay.
She got call waiting
call tracing
redialing
call blocking
one-way
two-way
three-way
please pray
for Nona Mae.

Leola Mae

Leola Mae is that wife with something to say,
but during dinner parties her Husband Ray
say she's had too much wine.
This he whispers in her ear
because truth be told,
Husband Ray knows
it ain't the wine that's driving Leola Mae.
It's a deep passion for a life long lived,
an intelligence long honed,
and a love still roaming
in her old bones that make
their dinner guests say,
"What a lovely wife, that Leola Mae."
So Leola pretend it's the wine
and hushes her mouth and
smiles in all the right places
as Ray carries on with his big hand
around her cold shoulder.
Leola Mae is tired.
Leola Mae tired.

Ruthie Mae

Now, you see that cat laying out
on the street?
That's a junkie.
Now, you can smoke a little weed if you want.
You can even drink a little rum
'cuz if you get real drunk
and fall down in the street,
you can get right up, go in the house,
take a bath, put on a nice pressed dress,
and come back out
and be Miss Jackson again.
But if you go the other way,
you cain't never get up, Ruthie.
No, no, no, you cain't never get up.

Betty Mae

This is what Betty Mae's got to say
about her tomorrows:
"You think the 1960s were something?
You just wait 'til the late 1990s.
Ever wonder
why we havin' the biggest military buildup
in this country's history
and there ain't no real enemy no mo'?
Well, when they cut the welfare,
folk gon' start rioting and the National Guard gon' be ready.
You ain't seen nothin' like it.
It's gon' be the '30s and the '60s combined."
Rita say,
"Betty Mae, you is one uninformed woman."
But Betty Mae say,
"Ever wonder
why all the ghettos 'cross America surrounded by freeways?
It's 'cuz they gon' need to use 'em to encircle us 'fo they go
in for the kill. You watch and see."
Rita say uninformed.
But that's what Betty Mae say.

Dr. Georgia Mae decided to move her practice from the suburbs to the city to start seeing about a population that had grown a-plenty. Doc told all of her patients in suburbia not to be afraid to come see her in the city, but her patients did protest. They feared crime and long waits that could be quite messy schedule-wise if you think about it long and hard enough. "We're just busy," they said. Snippy. Doc agreed this new population would be different. Their schedules were not as busy as those in the suburbs. But even they needed a doctor with a conscience. And Georgia Mae was such a doctor.

Georgia Mae

Gladys Mae

Gladys Mae called her doctor
because she was one of those leaking women.
"Not to worry, Gladys Mae," said her doctor,
who was female and quite capable.
"Your vaginal flora is very normal,
but there is a term for your condition.
You have vaginal rhinorrhea. It's like a runny nose."
"When does it stop?" said Gladys Mae,
who had been surfin' on mini-pads
darn near all her life (it seemed).
"Menopause," Doctor said
and bid Gladys Mae well,
but not before tellin' her to think of her leaks
as lemon verbena raindrops.

Madeline Mae

Madeline Mae remembers
the first time she stopped smiling in photographs.
Well, maybe not exactly stopped smiling.
Her schoolgirl mouthful of teeth became
a womanly closed–lip grin that spoke slow it down, sista.
Not because she was about to retire.
Women in their late twenties rarely do.
No, this was different.
Madeline was growin' into a new dress
not so lacy;
a new hat
not so floppy;
a new jacket not so thin.
Madeline Mae was growin' . . .

Penny Mae

Now, how Penny Mae came to spending
her Christmas in Italy is anyone's guess,
but the girl said she had a good time.
Went to fancy churches with
fine stained glass, museums full of
pretty pictures, and this lil restaurant
where you ate what they gave you.
Mama Mia was makin' no specials
for nobody, you hear? Miss Penny say the food
was real good, too.
Say in Italy all the young folk walk 'roun'
dressed in black, high-fashion-like, and
guess what that chile brought us back?
Some sweet potato-chocolate jam! Wrapped in silver paper,
real pretty-like. Ain't seen nothin' like it in all my days.
Never had the nerve to take it out the package,
but I'll call you when I do, you hear? I'll call you.

Lina Mae

Lina Mae was not your typical lady.
She was the party-maker. Played the perfect hostess
in a fine townhouse in Harlem.
Now, when other women were wearing
long skirts and corsets, Miss Lina had on
big britches made of silk that flowed
real nice when she sashayed in front of all her men friends.
She was always careful to serve hor d'oeuvres made
with only the finest meats and cheeses.
All kinda folk stopped in for her card games:
poets, singers, and movie stars.
Between hands, they danced to Ellington.
Now, they say she's even had some kings and queens
from Africa up in there and might be some truth to that
because Miss Lina know she know how to throw a good party.

April May hid out in a cabin in Maine so she could finish the world's greatest novel. Now, there was nobody her color for miles and miles around, but April made herself comfortable. Had a nice old couple from Carolina fixing her meals, organic greens and the like. The ole man was an I-talian who did pottery and wrote poems. The ole lady made a mean quilt and loved to tell stories about her ancestors from England, but took real pride in pointing out she had black blood in her veins, even though a certain great-aunt of hers could hardly entertain the notion. When she was a little girl, the lady would always ask her people why one of the women in the family photo album had hair a lil curlier than the others. And this particular aunt would hush her right quick and holler, "Maid!" And course this pretty woman in the family picture book was not the maid but the daughter of somebody who went astray, and this was something this ole lady in Maine took pride in to show her liberal bent. Miss April took it all in and smiled. At least they were connecting, and that was a start.

April May

Lissett Caballero said "ain't" in all the right places to fit in good with the black kids in her neighborhood. The brothers thought her accent was very lovely and after school the sisters would take turns plaiting Lissett's long black hair on the courtyard porch steps. Her papa was an artist from Cuba, but Mama was a high-brow from Colombia, where peacocks roamed the countryside and pretty birds sang at noon. This is what Lissett told the brother who would become her one and only. She charmed him with big pots of black beans and rice and a rather special coconut flan. They had pretty brown babies and moved to Louisiana, where he got a job on an oil rig. She only became a Mae after his people saw Miss Lissett could hum <u>Amazing Grace</u> as good as the rest of 'em. Hola.

Lissett Mae

Nelly Mae

Duke was Miss Nelly's common-law husband.

She use to help him down on his farm.

That is, when she wasn't up and down the streets,

working at the liquor store or the liquor bar.

Nelly loved her some liquor stores and liquor bars.

Course she had a cute shape

and could make a lot of tips.

One day she told Duke she was leavin' for a bit.

Had plans to go work for Jake Thomas.

Now, Duke didn't fight her 'cuz Nelly Mae

was known to do what she wanted to do. And this time she

was goin' out to the Gulf, where Ole Jake was building

a new bar.

Every day she would say, "I'm going out to the Gulf,

where Jake Thomas at." She went out to the Gulf alright,

but didn't stay too long. No, m'am.

Nell say she was 'fraid of them hurricanes

and brought her butt right back.

Now she talkin' 'bout openin' a juke joint.

Y'all want to help with the curtains?

Hilda Mae

Presently, in came the mama of the cottage,

Miss Hilda Mae Bohannon,

who knew everybody's business.

Could tell you who punched

in whose time card to make their check a lil fatter,

who had more wine than was necessary

at the company Christmas party,

and whose skirt could stand the hem being let down a bit.

But everybody loved them some Hilda.

She got the payroll sheets in on time,

offered a tip now and then

on how to make your expense account

work better for you ('cuz it wasn't her money),

and always had the right remedy for your summer cold.

Warm Vernors and some catnip tea would do it.

Now, Hilda always had a lil radio on her desk

and when a certain song by the O'Jays came on,

she would hop up from her desk

and get a lil groove goin'. Just a lil one.

Didn't want to scare the company CEO too much.

The kids called Renada White Girl all through grade school 'cuz she talked more proper than was allowed. And to make matters worse, she got all A's. Read Plato like it was poetry and talked 'bout how she gon' be a rocket scientist when she grew up. But on the day that Cynthia Crawford and Richelle Brown announced that they were going to make up a dance for the sixth-grade talent show, Renada wanted in. If they would only give her a chance, she was gon' show them that she too had some shake in her bake. Now Cynt and 'Chelle sneered at the idea, but obliged Miss Renada, who showed up to rehearsal on time every day. Even brought her big brother's boom box to score some brownie points. And on the day the lights went low, Renada took center stage and got down, got down like a clown. I'm tellin' you, the girl got down.

Renada Mae

Esther Mae

"I been thinkin'," Esther Mae said.
"I been thinkin' 'bout how things turned out . . .
Oh, in the past week. Months. Years . . .
Walk? Yes, I walk.
I read, do plenty of reading.
But I been thinkin', too."
On a trip to Montana she wore a mink.
When she got there, she called the bellboy feeble-minded
'cuz he forgot one of her bags.
Always did look like she belonged
on the cover of <u>Essence.</u>
And last night her husband told her as much.
"She still beautiful," he said, lookin' at her
rockin' in that ole chair by the window.
"She still beautiful."

May Desíree

May Desiree delights in knowing
that her walk is just right
but her talk is polite
because her mama raised a lady.
To all the brothers who would call at her
she begs for some understanding.
"Would you like somebody talkin'
to yo' lil sista like that?" she says
gently. The brothers grin at her
and move along.
And Miss Desiree gets on to her dance class,
taking time to smile at the Korean lady
who sell roses up on the corner.

Mama Mae

Mama Mae put three children through college,
one through graduate school,
with card games in her basement.
See, Mama and her friends switched up houses
for these games.
Took a few months before
they got to our house, but when they did,
the host kept some of the pot
and could even make mo' money on the side
by serving dinners. Mama made a mean pound cake.
Even the kids got in on the action by making runs
to the corner store for cigarettes, chewing gum, and pop.
I always saved my money,
and one year I bought Mama a pretty bangle.

Angel Mae

I asked my angel what she look like
and she told me, "Quite unlike any you've ever seen."
So I asked my angel to help me draw her
and she told me to pick up a magazine.
And so I'm flipping and flapping through
the pages and my eyes fall on a rather
blonde baby wearing a Prada peacoat and
I told my Angel Mae, "Surely you jest."
But she said, "G'on, girl, and try me."
And so I do. And my angel be stylin'
and profilin' like none you've ever seen.

Mary Mae

They call Miss Mary Bahama Mama,
but she ain't from Nassau
or even Eleuthera.
She from Miss'sippi, if you can believe it.
Queen of the Goombay, her conch dishes
outsell 'em all. Pretty shells and fish nets
and flowers flank her table and when the
Junkanoo come jookin' down the street,
playing that island music,
Mama take her spatula and get out wit 'em
and dance in place.
I say, "Miss Mary, how you come to learnin'
'bout these island people?"
And she told me, "My daughter married a Bahamian
and his people learned her the recipes and she learned me
and I added my own good sense to the lot
and that's how Bahama Mama came to be."
And I say, "Mama, shake it."

Yali Mae went to see the Stone Lady today. Being that she's the daughter of a Pentecostal preacher, she knew it was the work of the devil, but she was married now. And her daddy didn't know anyway. Miss Stone Lady was a trim lil somethin' in her forties. Wore white sandals. Probably watched _Oprah_ every day. Miss Stone Lady invited Yali in to sit a spell. Then Miss Stone Lady closed her eyes and finally said, "Somebody has you in their prayers," and Yali knew it was her mama. Mama was always praying for somebody. Next thing Yali know, the lady start tellin' her 'bout some past life in Normandy. Yali say, "Africa would've been better, but what choo gon' do?" Say the lady told her that her family in that lifetime traveled to parties in all kinda places — China, Europe and Japan, even Africa — and Yali was a cute lil thing who mingled well with the upper crust. But there was one problem: she had a lil brother who always got sick. Yali was fit to be tied, figurin' that he was doin' it with intentions, but one day the lil fella got so sick, he died. In time, Yali's mind went bad on her. Not even the tea them Chinese monks gave her could help her. One morning they found her heaped over in a chair, dead. Say she choked on a piece of meat. Now, y'all know Yali don't eat steak today outta fear it'll kill her, but she didn't tell the Stone Lady that. No, she just paid the lady her fee and went on home and thought about it all for a good long while.

Yali Mae

Etienne Mae

Etienne, Etienne, tell me your story
of how you left Port-au-Prince with your baby on your back.
Etienne, Etienne, tell me your story
of how you clung to the side of that boat
when the water looked like a better cradle.
Of how you settled in Miami in a little room on 82nd Street.
Washing clothes in hotel basements, living on rice and beans,
singing songs from the old land while you
rocked your baby fast to sleep.
Etienne, Etienne, tell me your story
of how you set up a booth at the Farmer's Market
and sold fancy turbans for people to wear and how in two years
you had a lil blue Toyota and a new perm in your hair.
How you always thought of Aunt Marie, little Pascal, and
Jean. How you sent boxes
home to them filled with pretty skirts, nice shoes, and
other things. How you danced
by the moonlight and held your head up high — high! How you
lit a candle by
morning and knew everything was gon' be alright.
Etienne, Etienne, tell me your story.

Ole Miss Maybell

Hey, y'all,

look here.

Here come Ole Miss Maybell,

pushing that dumb cart down the street.

"I know what they sayin',

what they sayin' 'bout me.

Figure I don't know how to do nuthin'

but push this ole cart down the street.

Been 'round many a day,

been to the river and seen many a thing.

Some figure I might as well be dead,

since all I do is push this ole cart down the street.

Don't know nuthin' 'bout where I been,

don't know nuthin' 'bout me.

All they see is these ribbons in my hair

and me pushin' this ole cart down the street."

What-ch'all figure Miss Maybell got in that ole cart?

I be trying to look, but cain't never see.

She always got that pretty purple blanket thrown 'cross it so,

tryin' to make like she got somethin' to see.

Now, comin' up, Nita had the benefit of Miss Sylvia and her husband, Tommy Lee. They were some good people who lived 'cross the street. Took interest in lil Nita 'cuz her parents were always on the road, followin' the crops. Miss Sylvia never was able to have children, so Nita was the perfect pick. They paid for her piano lessons and on occasion bought her fancy dresses. And Miss Nita Mae charmed them by gettin' good grades and makin' it on time to Sunday school every week. One year she even went to the state capital to compete in the spelling bee. Her parents were just tickled.

Nita Mae

Bay Mae

Mama called me the other day
to tell me 'bout lil Miss Bay Mae.
Say Miss Thing got up 'bout midnight
one night, talkin' 'bout "Grandma! Grandma!"
Singin' "Grandma! Grandma!"
Good mornin' to you.
We're all in our places
with bright shining faces.
"Grandma, how come
yo' face ain't shining?
Grandma, sing!"
I say, "Lord, what we gon' do wit' her?"

Olivia Mae

There's a little girl in our building. Her name is Olivia Mae.
She's quite coy, but sincere when she says, "Have a nice day."
She peeps around the corner before she says hello. If you invite
her in for tea,
she asks, "Should I bring my piccolo?"
She likes going through my bras. They're quite lacy —
like her mother's.
And if I'm on the phone too long, out of my guest room
she will come,
dressed in pearls and feathers. I say, "Miss Olivia! What a
dame you are.
Your lipstick is just right. My brother, Roberto, just called.
He's coming over tonight. Would you care to stay for dinner
and charm him with
your waves?" And Miss Olivia, with a sexy grin, will whisper,
"I would love to, darlin', but I must go upstairs
where a bubble bath awaits me.
And after that my raspberry tea. Then on to my room and
into my bed,
where Mommy says I must be so she can spend the evening
with our Uncle Frankie." So I bid Miss Olivia good-bye,
but not before I ask her to think of yellow brick roads
in faraway places
where birds and animals sing songs of sunny days,
sweepin' clouds away.
Then I give her a hug and tell her, "Sweet dreams."

About the Author and Illustrator

Sharony Andrews Green, 30, is a journalist and the former Assistant National Editor at the Detroit Free Press. A Miami native and former reporter for The Miami Herald, Green has a special fondness for the name Mae and its presence in her upbringing and familial roots. She's always wanted to mix words with her first love, drawing.